The Accidental Shaman

A beautifully satirical origin story about a warthog who never meant to become a guru.

By Lora W. Dail

Illustrated by RAM Shamanai
(well, imagined by Lora, interpreted by RAM, and occasionally hijacked by Mudwhiff)

MUDWHIFF THE ACCIDENTAL SHAMAN

ISBN: 979-8-9991424-7-4

Enter at Your Own Risk:

This is a work of fiction sprung from wildy imaginative minds. Any resemblance to actual warthogs, gurus, influencers, celestial beings, or myths is either completely coincidental—or wildly inevitable, depending on your perspective.

Please enter at your own risk. There should be no physical danger, but your mind may expand, and your heart may open. You may also experience laughter, insight, and muddy joy.

You've been warned.

Trademark Acknowledgment:

Amazon, Apple, Burning Man, ChatGPT, CrossFit, DOS, Evian, Instagram, Kodak, Nerf, TED Talks, TikTok, Vogue, Volkswagen, Zork, and *The Cha Cha Slide* are trademarks or copyrights of their respective owners. These names are referenced within this work for descriptive and/or satirical purposes with the utmost respect.

No affiliation, sponsorship, or endorsement is intended or implied.

All rights remain with the original trademark holders—with our thanks for being so big, their names became household words (and references in warthog fables). We hope they accept our use with the respect it's intended—and maybe even a knowing grin of pride.

Desert Vogue is a fictional, satirical creation and is in no way affiliated with the iconic *Vogue* or Condé Nast. Although, let's be honest... Mudwhiff's cover is stunning, and we could totally see him on the real Vogue!

Invitation to our Reader...

They say you must strive to 'Become.' Work hard. Study. Pray. Fast. Align your chakras. Shed your ego. Grow your own herbs.

But did you ever stop to wonder... become what, exactly?

You've been taught that you need to become something, when maybe... you already are.

What if you were worthy before the workshop? Magnificent before the mantras. Fabulous before the fasting.

What if you really believed, like we do, that you are:

- Beautiful.
- Full of potential.
- Worthy of your dreams.
- Perfect (or perfectly imperfect).
- Already enough.

And what if Mudwhiff isn't the only one with a dream?

So, get comfortable. Maybe a soft blanket and your feet up. And definitely snacks.

Then root in, dear reader, and proceed with reverence and curiosity.

Because, while this story may be about our humble warthog, Mudwhiff... you might just see yourself.

With our love,

from the brave, the glittering, and the mildly muddy (in any order)

Lora, RAM, and Mudwhiff

The Desert Speaks

I have been here since before.

Before borders. Before names.

Before the warthogs wallowed and the geckos barked.

When there was water, and I was underwater.

There was a time I moved freely.

Today, I am still. Held in place by time itself.

I am the Desert. And boy, do I have stories.

My oldest companions are the Stars, the Moon, and the Sun. We've whispered secrets across eons. The Moon speaks in circles; cryptic, contemplative, nosy, and a little co-dependent. The Sun? Always punctual, slightly dramatic, can be shady. The Stars? Bright and surprising.

Together, we've seen it all: the comings, the goings, the civilizations that refused to hydrate. The Sun counts their moments, the Moon counts their days, and the Stars count their months. And me? I hold their lives.

We have tried to share our Wisdom; our Secrets. Twice. Quite unsuccessfully.

And now we watch the new ones. So different from any others.

They've released themselves from the surface.

Something always up above: planes, starships, space houses.

Now satellites litter the ceiling, beaming beams of beamable things.

Chasing Likes and followers through yoga poses and digital retreats. Hoarding hashtags and content like the most important discoveries discovered.

We know Truth. Did I mention we've tried to share our Truth?

We have. Twice.

and speaks, and speaks…

First, Dinosaurs. Big mistake. All they wanted was more ferns. They forgot the whole point: to grow into greatness, not gorge on greens. They stomped, chomped, and chaos-ed their way out of the picture, with a little help from the Stars.

Next, we told the Water People. They got carried away, literally, with their own importance. Forgot the Source. The Moon took care of them. Swimmingly, we might add.

We recently thought: "Perhaps it's time to try again. And this time, the Animals."

But which?

Elephants? Good size, smart. But so busy remembering things.

Meerkats? Cute. Social. But way too much drama.

Owl? Good choice, very wise. But owl pellets. Ewww.

We worked through the animal kingdom, alphabetically, with no success… until "W."

Warthog. Warthog? Well, wait a minute now…

Warthog is tenacious. Persistent. Adaptable. Brave. Mud-loving.

He snorts. He wallows. He roots. He listens.

He loves the mud, which makes me happy. He hangs out during the day, which pleases the Sun, but sometimes comes out at night to avoid the heat of the day, which tickles the Moon and the Stars to no end.

And Warthog is not beautiful. No, not that! Or huge. But present. And real.

And so, it was decided: Warthog. And in time, we selected an oddly enlightened, blissfully grounded warthog named Mudwhiff.

You'd think, for all of our wisdom, that we would foresee the events we were about to set into motion.

Funny… we did not.

Just a Warthog

Mudwhiff was a simple pig. With a simple life.

A wife he loved and a life he enjoyed.

He was a warthog with a vision, though. While he cherished the beauty of his desert home, he dreamed of a place of abundance. Green, lush, vast. Where the word "lack" was a stranger. Where water never disappeared. Where fruits fell from trees and all animals easily found food. Where a hot warthog could find the coolest, smoothest mud the very moment he wanted. Mudwhiff dreamed of an oasis in the desert.

He carried his dream like a secret, sheltered from the ones who had mocked it. But Mudwhiff believed in his dream, his Oasis. And quietly, stubbornly, he held on to the possibility. Not sure how, but sure, nonetheless.

Until *that* day came, Mudwhiff went about his regular life. He woke in his burrow, snuggled up with his wedded wartsow.

Their very first act? A good morning kiss. An awkwardly tender, time-consuming testament to their years of love. Of maneuvering tusks, warts, and lips into a place that even allowed a kiss to happen. But every morning, maneuver they did, and every morning, with grunts, they began the day with a tender warthog "I love you."

So begins this day. Mudwhiff exits his burrow with a snort of thanks, not elegant, but earnest. He greets the sun with a nod of appreciation for it showing up. He nuzzles his favorite acacia tree, not to eat, just to say hello. He waits patiently for ants to cross his path, offering a polite, possibly snarky, "Excuse me," as they pass.

At the quiver tree, when the pied crows are near, he lets them work his back and head, plucking off the night's uninvited hitchhikers. A perfect transaction; pest control for him, a morning snack for the crows. Both sides happy (except for the hitchikers).

With grateful grunts, Mudwhiff did his dailies without complaint; because every chore, every ant sidestep, and every crow negotiation brought him that much closer to his favorite part of the day: the sacred, squishy glory of his afternoon wallow.

Scent and Significance

Mudwhiff never rushed to his waterhole, preferring instead to saunter in, savoring the journey as much as the destination. He always respected the others who came, not like the oryx, who chased everyone off, or the gnus, who'd just step on you without noticing. He did enjoy the jackals, though, their tails wagging, always playful.

Before wallowing, Mudwhiff always enjoyed a long drink (a fellow has to hydrate, you know). Sometimes he would sink onto his knees to make the sipping simpler.

And then, honoring the sacred-but-silly code etched in his DNA, it was time to squish, swirl, and terraform. Creating the *best* wallow a warthog had ever known, at least for that day.

If it was hot, he'd dig deep for cooler mud.

If it rained, he'd enjoy the puddles.

Whatever the day brought, he'd adapt without complaint.

It wasn't performance. It was presence.

He simply *was*, content and crusty, because he was Mudwhiff.

But remember: Appreciation sends out vibrations. And Gratitude echoes far.

The Sun felt it. The Desert noticed and told the Stars. And the Moon, of course, heard, and saw, everything.

And so, a decision was made. Mudwhiff was chosen. A stage was set.

This afternoon, as the sun angled its golden spears across the dunes, Mudwhiff got busy sniffing and rooting out the perfect wallow.

Searching for mud that was sticky with purpose and squishy with potential.

Today, he was under the impression that he had chosen his wallow himself, not realizing he was being led to a metaphorical X that marked a very particular spot.

Preparing the Portal

A scent, layered and strange enticed him. A tang of distant storms.

A whisper of flowers his brain didn't recognize. The scent hummed with something he didn't have words for. The soil shimmered beneath his hooves, pulsing with a quiet invitation. This was no ordinary patch of dirt. This was something special.

A place the Stars had marked.

Mudwhiff tilted his head, puzzled by such a strange and oddly poetic thought.

Prophetically, a vision of his Oasis shimmered in his mind.

He shook his head to clear it. "Must be hot out here today," he muttered.

A big, male oryx wandered past, giving Mudwhiff the side-eye. Mudwhiff, deep in his wallow work, didn't notice, or didn't care. A barking gecko tiptoed behind the oryx (easy for a tiny, unreasonably loud lizard) and screeched five times. The oryx panicked, kicked, lunged left, saw nothing… and ran away anyway, like destiny was chasing him. Or worse: an ex-girlfriend from 260 days ago.

Mudwhiff chuckled as he always did at this game. Hinge, his best gecko, had no love for the proud, prancing oryx. "National animal, my barking hiney," he'd scoff, every time one trotted past waving its precious horns.

Their laughter faded as they watched the oryx join its herd.

Mudwhiff stepped into the spot he'd chosen. He dropped onto his front knees and dug his powerful snout into the red mud. Slowly, reverently, he began to rearrange it; scooping, shaping, and sculpting patterns only he could see.

"This is not just a puddle. Not just a wallow," he whispered. "This is... well, it's perfection. No, this is *my* portal *to* perfection - absolutely the perfect place for today's muditation."

He chuckled, a rich, charming chortle that bubbled up like mischief in mud, proud of himself and the magnificent absurdity of being a most handsome, and modest, warthog who is both wise and punny.

The Sacred Snooze

Hinge ignored him. He'd heard this before. Every day of their friendship, in fact.

"Mud is proof the Universe loves us," was a documented Mudwhiffism.

But somehow Mudwhiff felt that today *was* special, the best wallow ever.

The mud. The desert. The quiet companionship of the waterhole.

He paused. Sat up like a curious dog. Perked his ears. Scented the air.

Scanned the horizon with his discerning, warty eyes.

Convinced all was well, he wiggled his bottom securely into the mud. He then, well, released, and melted down onto his belly with a long, satisfied grunt.

"Yeeessss…" he sighed aloud to no one in particular.

He then splorshed onto his side. Kicked his legs out and up, rolling his round sides into the mud up to his spine. A few times, as it takes a bit to coat a pig. (Have you ever spice-rubbed a pork butt? You get it.) He rolled to the other side and repeated the process.

"Mmmmm…." he sighed dreamily. "Perfection! This puddle will transform this hot, humble pig into a cool, crusty character faster than a piglet can spin. Mud Protection Factor 50 with better-than-DEET insect defense! This really is the portal to perfection!"

Mudwhiff wallowed. Kicked. Coated. And repeated the process. Several times.

For what felt like both five minutes and forever, he rolled and rooted.

And, as he was known to do, Mudwhiff drifted into a sound sleep mid-wallow.

Hinge barked and wandered home.

The Sun drifted down. The Moon began to rise. And far above, the Stars began to flicker on, just a little earlier than usual.

They all leaned in…

The Celestial Conference

"Alright everyone, this is it. Are we ready? Any doubts?"

"I sure did love the dinosaurs," lamented the Stars. "Not their fault, really. Those ferns were wildly psychotropic; turned all of them into wide-eyed leaf junkies. They clomped across continents high as pterodactyls, trying to eat volcanoes, chase clouds, and flirt with lightning bolts. It was chaos in scales, feathers, and thundering feet."

"Desert should have known," muttered the Moon.

"Sorry," said the Desert, not sorry at all. "I thought it was a harmless salad."

"I think we've picked well this time," said the Stars. "Mudwhiff is a simple creature. He's not huge. He's grounded. And most importantly, he lives in Namibia. It's the middle of nowhere. No offense, Desert."

"None taken," said the Desert. "We like our peace. And our obscurity. And frankly, no one visits unless they *really* mean to."

"That's true," said the Moon. "My Atlanteans had ambition and far too much reach. Their potential for destruction ranged wide. That could've ended badly."

"This desert is secluded, surrounded by mountains. If it goes sideways, few will even notice," said the Stars. "It's stunning, but isolated. We love shining here!"

"So, we agree. Shall we consult the orb?" asked the Stars. Everyone nodded.

A dark orb, etched with a white infinity symbol inside a circle, was produced and given a ceremonial shake. When the sphere settled, a message appeared: *"Yes. Signs point to yes."*

Celestial heads nodded solemnly, and the Desert added, "But this time, no ferns. No Sea Monkeys. And no glowing water temples, okay? Let's keep it grounded."

More nods. A shiver of unease.

And a quiet hope that this time… they'd get it right.

The Arrival of the Star

The decision took form in the cosmos and fell to Earth, forged in resolve, lit by prophecy, full of destiny and drama.

It inched its way across the sky, a sublime, slow-motion spectacle. It showered sparks and glitter like a tween's unicorn birthday party. It left a rainbow trail across the heavens. And it landed right where it was aimed, smack dab in the middle of Mudwhiff's wallow.

The impact was *glorious!* Mud bombs the size of bowling balls flew for hundreds of feet in all directions! A *BOOM* shot across the stillness, slammed the mountains, bounced back, hit itself midair, and did it again. It was the sound of a truth bomb being dropped. Thunder with reverb. Echo with attitude.

The valley was covered in stardust and sound, announcing that something sacred had shifted. Who would imagine it was a warthog, awakened.

When the last globs had globbed, and the last booms had boomed, all that remained was a crater the size of a small German car and a glowing swirl of purple-green star mud.

And buried, somewhere, under the glowing, globbing mud, was Mudwhiff.

"That was a bit much, wasn't it?" Desert and Moon asked the Stars simultaneously.

The Stars just shrugged.

Eyewitness Account

Gerald sat on the outdoor patio of a nearby eco-lodge, a birdwatcher-turned-journalist. He was half drunk on Namibian whiskey, embellishing life stories to a hottie named Fran and a group of travel influencers.

Trying to impress with his camera when the shooting star shot.

Gerald snapped seven pictures.

None were in focus. All were award-winning.

The headline read: "CELESTIAL SWINE SWAT: Warthog Gets a Wallop!"

Glowing, Speaking, Changing

Mudwhiff emerged from the Volkswagen-sized crater one week later.

Mud-slicked. Slightly concussed. Glowing.

He pulsed with a soft purple-green light that wrapped his body like moonlit fog. Star-mud orbs had fused into his mane like gemstone beads in braids, each one humming faintly with a frequency that felt 'more than.'

A strange, spiral tattoo shimmered on his flank, etched with an eerie precision, curling inward to form a single, perfect star.

It hadn't been there before.

He blinked at the world as if seeing it through new eyes; maybe he was… as his eyes were swirling, shimmering seas of cosmic dust and galaxies.

He didn't recognize a thing.

Not the mud. Not the desert.

Not even Hinge, who had sat vigil for the seven days.

Mudwhiff staggered once, righted himself, and began muttering softly:

"Transformation is dirty." "You shouldn't have to dig *that* deep for change." "A Portal to Perfection is always nearby."

Then, still glowing, still dazed, Mudwhiff staggered off into the darkness.

The gecko fainted.

The Moon screamed.

The Desert just smiled and said, "Well, here we go again."

No one expected anything to have happened to the wallow, but it did.

ORGANIC
TEAS

The Boutique Awakening

The next morning, just after breakfast, the automatic doors of the nearby eco-lodge whispered open with a soft chime, and in strolled Mudwhiff.

Still glowing. Still fog-wrapped. Still muttering mantras.

Heads turned. Forks froze mid-air. One guest choked on an elderberry.

Mudwhiff didn't seem to notice. His hooves clicked against the polished concrete floor as if he'd always walked upright. The spiral tattoo on his flank had morphed, multiplied, and moved. He walked directly into the boutique.

Without hesitation, he grabbed a batiked sarong and whipped it around his waist with the practiced grace of a yogi.

Then, with the solemnity of a pilgrim selecting a sacred relic, he chose a strand of oversized mala beads because they felt "vibrate-y." He maneuvered them over his tusks, warts, ears, and bedazzled mane with reverent precision.

And then, because he was, after all, still a warthog, he snagged an organic dark chocolate bar from a display, ripped the package open with his tusk, and began munching as he wandered to the exit.

The manager and the cashier shook themselves from Mudwhiff's spell and charged after him, yelling something about shoplifting. Mudwhiff paused, turned slowly, and blinked at them with wide, shimmering eyes. With chocolate still smudged across his snout, he whispered reverently:

"Beloved bean of divine bitterness... you are the shadowed light in my soul's desert."

"Daaaang, he's good," someone whispered from the incense display.

Somewhere, a crystal in the gift shop began to hum.

Mudwhiff strolled out the door, still glowing, still muttering, still munching.

A legend was born. And he'd accessorized it himself.

His First Follower

"I've got it! I'll pay for it! Please, just charge it to my room!"

A woman in gauzy linen pants, sunglasses the size of moons, a floppy hat, and an aura of Amazon abundance and 5G satisfaction sprinted across the lobby, eager to encounter this oddly magnetic, glowing figure now traipsing from the gift shop like the prophecy no one pre-ordered.

"Let's have a matcha," she said, steering Mudwhiff toward the outdoor café.

"Matcha would be *wonderful,*" Mudwhiff replied, licking chocolate from his tusk with profound dignity, slightly curious if matcha was food.

Her name was Sol.

She had been to Bali.

She had been to Burning Man.

She had been to therapy (twice).

And now, she had found Him. Mudwhiff. Looking sort of like a warthog, if warthogs wore sarongs and beads and dreads. Speaking like a mystic.

Lit up like a disco ball that had just wallowed in glitter.

Everything in her carefully curated, over-filtered life clicked.

"This is it," she thought. "The answer! The vibe! The brand!" She drooled.

A warthog in a sarong. A fabulously righteous creature. She was already basking in her adjacent viralness. "What happened to you? Make it profound," she prompted him, pulling out her phone.

Mudwhiff blinked. Swallowed. Pondered *'profound'* and responded very slowly. Agonizing silence stretched between each word. Each syllable perfectly articulated:

"Mud. Sleep. Star. Matcha."

Hashtags, video, post and "The Warthog Way" was born.

"If you can't see the light...
you're too deep in the mud."

THE
WARTHOG
WAY

#MudWhiffdom
#RootYourTruth

THE
WARTHOG
WAY

Eyewitness Account (part two)

Gerald, fresh from the fame of his award-winning photos and a five-day bender, stumbled back to the eco-lodge. Hungover, sunburned, and mildly philosophical, he looked up from his espresso and saw… Mudwhiff.

Wearing a sarong. Holding a smoothie. Quoting Lao Tzu.

Gerald blinked three times and Mudwhiff remained. He lifted his camera, snapped four photos, sent them to his editor, muttered, "I need to lay down," and passed out in a beanbag chair made from recycled safari uniforms.

Gerald's photos were featured with an article titled, "CELESTIAL SWINE: Warthog or Cosmic Oracle? Namibia Goes Hog Wild!"

Rise of the Warthog

Sol's matcha video hit 2.1 million views before lunch. Gerald's photos and Sol's hashtags created a perfect storm that brought hordes of the seeking to the desert. On day three, Mudwhiff and The Warthog Way went viral.

Followers and seekers flooded the eco-lodge. They came with yoga mats, sage sticks, homemade vision boards, and ring lights. There were smoothies. There were selfies. There were influencers. There was patchouli.

Mudwhiff, saint of the sacred swine, had added a second sarong and offered gems like: "If you can't see the light, you're too deep in the mud." And "True serenity should be sought in threes: you must wallow your soul, crust your body, and evict your parasites."

Hashtags erupted: #Mudwhiffdom #RootYourTruth #SacredStuff and #MudwhiffSaidIt

Mudwhiff wallowed.

In praise.

In adulation.

In swag.

DESERT VOGUE

Wallowing
in Bed Keeps
the Mrs. Happy

Mudwhiff
How Does
Wallowing
Compare with
the Kama Sutra?
OUR EXPERTS DISCUSS

Authenticity
Is the New Filter

Too Much Star, Not Enough Pig

The throng drove Range Rovers into the desert where Mudwhiff performed a dance challenge on a dune with a trio of influencers while quoting Rumi and chewing kale.

He orchestrated a scare prank on Sol with a strategically placed beetle and a wildebeest mask that received 4.7 million views. Before dinner.

They held a Sunset Gratitude Stampede, where followers galloped in slow motion across the dunes chanting, "I receive!" into the wind while misting each other with essential oils infused with desert essence and light codes.

Mudwhiff even posed for a *Desert Vogue* photo shoot titled: "Warts & Peace: The Bold Beauty of Becoming." He wore seven layered sarongs and a crown of ethically gathered peacock beetle shells. One photo was captioned: "Authenticity is the new filter." Another: "Leave no trace, except your impact."

They held impromptu Individuality Celebrations, where seekers flung sacred dirt at each other to honor "the beautiful oneness of uniqueness."

Every day began at sunrise with Moans and Grunts, a communal vocal awakening to realign the chakras. At sunset, hundreds gathered to shout thank yous into the canyon so they would echo into the oncoming night. These were often layered with grateful wails and intentional weeping.

Hilariously, both Moon and Sun were equally annoyed.

There were so many hashtags the dunes themselves began to crumble under the sheer spiritual weight of it all.

And over at their burrow, Mrs. Mudwhiff had had enough.

She sent Hinge on a mission.

The Cha Cha Slide

Hinge arrived at the lodge and froze: it was almost unrecognizable. There were impromptu drum circles, spontaneous mud wallows, uncontrollable uploading, and a suspicious number of gongs. He caught Mudwhiff on the meditation deck, glowing with overexposure.

"Pigman," Hinge barked pleadingly. "You need to come home. You need help."

Mudwhiff turned, smiling with the gentle confusion of someone who's stared too long into the cosmos or a ring light. "I am the help, buddy. Just ask them." With that, Mudwhiff stepped onto the stage, his glittering sarong catching the light.

"Hey, everyone, listen close! Did you know that all of us, every single one of us, is woven together like music. You're a part of me. I'm a part of you. And the whole wild world is dancing inside of us." *slide to the right*

Puzzled faces smiled and nodded, hidden behind their livestreaming phones.

slide to the left "So today," Mudwhiff star-splained, "let's generate some gratitude and embrace realness by wallowing, with deep, soul-satisfying joy, in the sacred mud of transformative perfection, where it all started!"

Puzzled faces puzzled harder, viewer counts soared higher, and hashtags bloomed like desert flowers. *cha cha real smooth*

Mudwhiff hit Warrior Pose, grunted three times, then executed a perfect swan dive/belly flop fusion into a kiddie pool filled with red dirt and Evian.

Mud flew. People screamed. Sacred sludge flew fifty feet in every direction. And the crowd? They lost their minds, swooning ecstatically, cha-cha'ing enthusiastically, and swan diving into their own personal portals to perfection.

When the mud cleared, all that Hinge could see were phones and rear ends waving in the air to a peppy Latin rhythm. He barked and turned away.

The Desert let out a long, low sigh that skimmed the dunes as a whisper, sounding suspiciously like, "So very close…"

Mrs. Mudwhiff Speaks

Hinge was reporting back to Mrs. M. as she stepped outside. Everything felt off, made worse with the irksome scent of influencer on the breeze. Her warts twitched.

"So, he's over there, glowing and carrying on, is he?" Mrs. Mudwhiff asked out loud.

"Yes, but not with purpose," the Sun vented.

"He didn't get it, he didn't get the why," the Moon whined. "And his latest mantra rhymed, Desert. It *rhymed!*"

"We overdid it," stated the Stars. "We may just have to cut our losses and start over."

Hearing this, Mrs. Mudwhiff's tail shot up. Her mane flared. She spun in three impossibly tight circles, stopped in a storm of dust, and stomped all four hooves.

"You will do no such thing. That is MY husband and he's YOUR responsibility. You geniuses broke him. You FIX him!"

From behind a dune, Hinge barked his assent. He was as tired of Mudwhiff's symphonic sound baths as the next guy, but he was not about to lose his friend to celestial incompetence. He barked again, emphatically.

The Moon, the Stars, the Sun, and the Desert huddled, whispering across the sky, all shimmering hush and cosmic static. Eventually, a decision.

With a ***vhoohp,*** a soft leather pouch materialized in Mrs. M.'s surprised hand. The bag was adorned with celestial sequins, colorful crystals, and otherworldly sigils.

POP. A glowing, opalescent Magic Grub appeared and dropped inside.

POP. Two more wiggling grubs materialized and tumbled in, holding hands.

POP. A fourth appeared, grinning as it fell into the pouch.

The grubs began to hum. A low, mysterious, oddly bass-toned, interstellar harmony; equal parts whale song, prophecy, and slightly off-key ukuleles.

"Feed him these," the Desert whispered. "He will remember."

#PowerCoupleVibes 💜
She said *'in* a wallow' and I FELT that
✨WALL'O'W ENERGY✨
Okay but why am i jealous??

The Talk and The Walk

Hinge pestered Mrs. Mudwhiff the entire walk to the resort, fretting about how they were supposed to get Mudwhiff away from the crowd.

"He's glowing! And they *like* the glow! He's talking like a mystic. And they *love* the talk. He's meditating… or levitating… or something. He's just *so much* right now. And they love the 'too much' him! He's not just going to leave all of that."

Mrs. Mudwhiff flicked her tail. "I'll handle it. Whatever you do, do not laugh."

Hinge muttered something about warthogs and theatrics but kept walking.

They found Mudwhiff in the lobby, creating affirmation cards between the Selfie Wall and the Build-a-Scent Essential Oil Bar. He was mid-snort-affirmation when he spotted them.

"Darling!" he beamed. "What a surprise!"

He turned to the group. "Everyone, this is my wife! And my friend, Hinge!"

Phones rose. Ring lights glowed. Shutters snapped.

"Hi, everyone," she said with a smile.

Then, she turned to Mudwhiff, eyes soft. "Darling, I have missed you. I really need to *uh*, talk, to you." *Beat*. "Alone. In a wallow. Please?" she batted her lashes.

Livestreams were age restricted. Viewership skyrocketed.

Hinge choked. This was not the Mrs. M. he knew! "Ahem. Perhaps, my friend… it is time for a walk?"

Mudwhiff choked. Blinked. Gulped. His glow deepened. Then he smiled. Deeply. "Why yes," he said slowly. "A wallow, er, a walk, sounds wonderful."

And just like that, they turned and walked out.

No goodbye post. No sayonara smoothie. Just hoof clicks, gecko tail drags. And silence.

"Well… that went better than I expected," Hinge muttered as they walked away.

The Absence of Mudwhiff

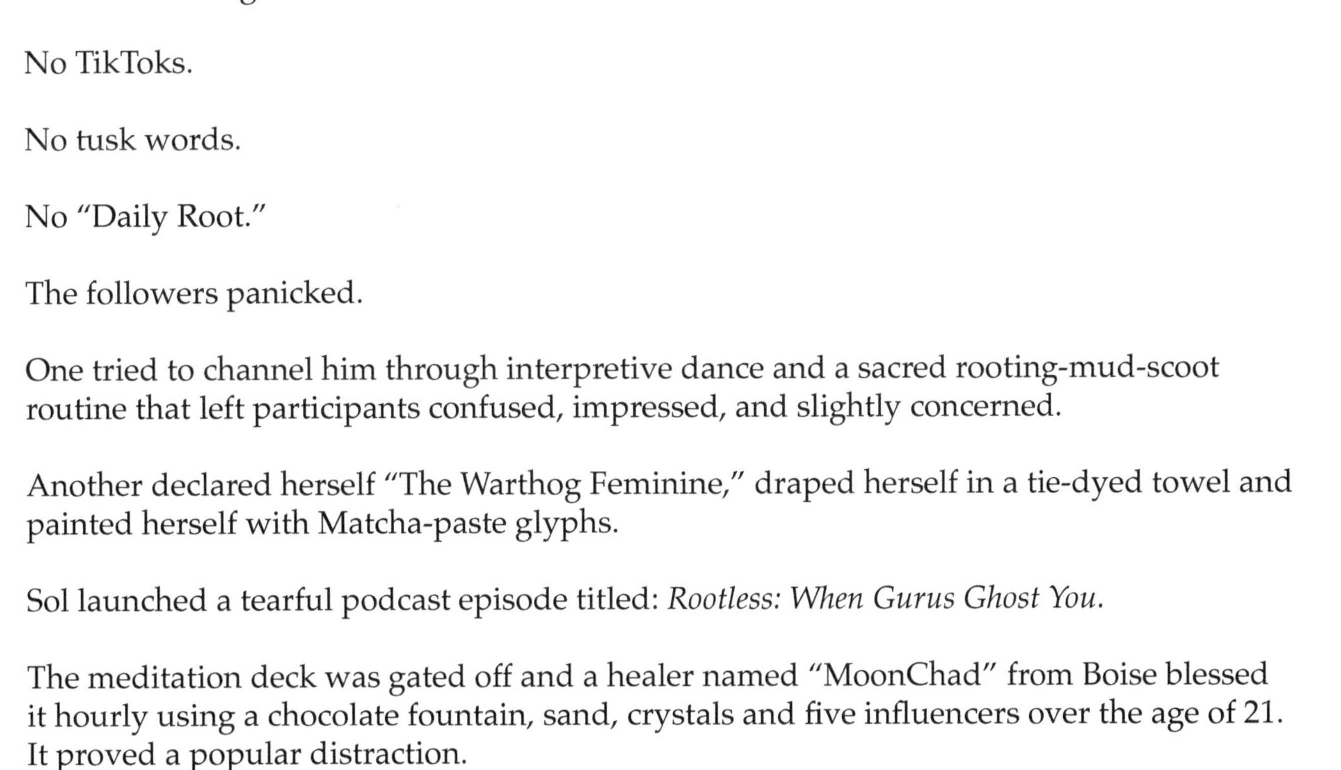

The lodge fell into chaos.

Mudwhiff was gone.

No TikToks.

No tusk words.

No "Daily Root."

The followers panicked.

One tried to channel him through interpretive dance and a sacred rooting-mud-scoot routine that left participants confused, impressed, and slightly concerned.

Another declared herself "The Warthog Feminine," draped herself in a tie-dyed towel and painted herself with Matcha-paste glyphs.

Sol launched a tearful podcast episode titled: *Rootless: When Gurus Ghost You.*

The meditation deck was gated off and a healer named "MoonChad" from Boise blessed it hourly using a chocolate fountain, sand, crystals and five influencers over the age of 21. It proved a popular distraction.

An emergency line of smoothies was released under the brand *Wallow Juice* with flavors like "Enlighten-Mint" and "Choco-Chakra Swirl."

A few loyalists tried to start a Mudwhiff Fan Club but quickly got bogged down in the naming. They were torn between "The Tusked," "The Gruntful," and "Mudwhiff's Mudheads." Their debate was heated, spiritual, and weirdly adjective-laden, with words like "warty," "sacred," and "unfiltered" entering the fray.

The Wi-Fi flickered.

The ring lights dimmed.

And somewhere in the dunes, the Desert chuckled up a dust storm.

Into the Red Dunes

Hinge and the warthogs disappeared into the red silence of Namibia… away from crowds, phones, and live streams. They took him back to where it all began: the waterhole. The one that had unintentionally absorbed a trace of Mudwhiff's dream in the star-smacking. It hadn't been a one-way download after all. A bit of Mudwhiff had slipped free and blueprinted the Oasis into being.

It was real: born of his dream. His longing. His becoming.

The waterhole had outgrown its name.

It now stretched wide enough to reflect the full arc of the moon.

It was longer than a redwood was tall. Deeper than a TED Talk. Bigger than ambition, smaller than grace. Deep enough to hold silence yet still enough to remember every truth whispered into it. A sacred mirror waiting for those ready to look inside.

Camelthorn trees with glowing leaves grew where none had before. Fruit trees flourished. Flowers bloomed. Grasses and shrubbery now adorned the desert floor.

And in the middle, a stunning star-fed spring — an Oasis, true and undeniable.

Mudwhiff staggered when he saw it. Gobsmacked. This was his Oasis.

* * *

Eventually, the Desert whispered: "It's time."

Mrs. Mudwhiff opened the leather pouch and shook the Magic Grubs into her palm. They tumbled out and sat, solemn and knowing. Aware their moment had arrived.

She passed the grubs to Mudwhiff reverently, a bit hesitant. Hinge looked on solemnly.

Mudwhiff blinked.

"Dinner?"

The gecko shook his head.

"Destiny."

The Grub-Induced Awakening (part one)

The Magic Grubs tasted like garlic and epiphany.

Mudwhiff fell into a dream. Or a vision. Or a very well-lit metaphor.

He floated in the sky, surrounded by swirling stars and soft whispers. And a voice:

> *You are not meant to be followed.*
> *You are meant to remind them of roots.*
> *Of belly-down, snout-to-earth joy.*
> *You are the example.*

The wind softened. The Stars leaned in.

The whispering voices melded and sang:

> *We are all one.*
> *Always be grateful.*
> *Leave the world better than you found it.*

Images began to flash… Knowledge from Before…

He saw the dinosaurs - thunder-footed and full of promise. But obsessed.

So concerned with *More* they never imagined *Better*. They did not build a Dinotopia for all, just chomped and stomped their way to extinction.

He saw the Atlanteans; blindingly beautiful and brilliant; mesmerized by the mere idea of themselves. Their towers collapsed beneath waves they forgot to honor.

The Moon sighed. The Stars dimmed. The Desert wept dry tears.

And Mudwhiff saw… the squandered promise. What could have been.

That was Then.

The Grub-Induced Awakening (part two)

Then he saw… himself. His awkward gait. His unkempt mane. His snorting laugh.

He heard the whispers he always heard:

"Not much to look at," from jackal. "That one? He's grey," the flamingo would scoff. "Dir-ty, dir-ty, dir-ty," from the guinea fowl.

Mudwhiff rejected the taunts as he awakened to the Truth: his humility was a gift, his warthogginess a blessing, and his immense gratitude a strength.

The vision shimmered like a mirage, and he saw the oasis. His Oasis.

Lush. Glowing. Welcoming. Not a fictional utopia, but a real place. Where all are welcome and all are appreciated. A place of plenty for everyone.

But something was missing. Not in the vision… in him.

He didn't see his place in it. He couldn't see how he fit in.

Then a voice boomed through the stars and into his vision, a warning and a promise.

The Oasis is not a gift.
It is a test made visible.
It will only remain if you face what is coming.

A powerful shiver of dread rippled through his Soul. And doubt… that a warthog should be chosen to face such a dire-sounding challenge.

But the vision shimmered again, to the Oasis, to his desert, to his life. To the potential of it all. The fear dissolved into dust, and he was left with warmth. With love. And resolve. That if he received a call, he would answer it bravely.

His snout wrinkled as a smile lifted his lips around his tusks. His eyes crinkled at the edges. Contented grunts escaped through the smile.

That was Then. This is Now. And the Future? It roots here.

With a smile on his face and resolve in his heart, Mudwhiff slept.

I release the followers and likes...
I release the swag and the curated
and the sponsored content!
I release the pressure
to sound profound!'

Letting Go

The next morning, Mudwhiff felt... *clear*.

Not glowing. Not concussed. Just... *aware*.

He dream-remembered the Joy he saw in his grub vision. The Love he shared, the Happiness he felt at the potential of the Future.

He walked over to where his wartsow still slept and sat next to her. He gently nudged her shoulder. When she awoke, he pulled her to him and began the awkward contortions that culminated in their grunty, good morning, 'I love you' kiss. Mudwhiff smiled. Mrs. M. smiled back.

"We begin here," he said softly.

He stood up, faced the wind, and shouted:

> *I release the followers and likes.*
> *I release the swag. the curated, and the sponsored content!*
> *I release the pressure to sound profound!*

The Sun smiled down on him and the Desert shifted in agreement.

Then, from across the dunes: a lion's roar.

Hinge shivered and stuttered, "Uh... is that real or a part of this releasing stuff?"

Mrs. Mudwhiff looked at her husband with concern. Mudwhiff raised an eyebrow and thought, "Well, *that* didn't take long."

He took a deep breath and exclaimed:

"Run!"

Hinge and Mrs. Mudwhiff didn't wait. They scrambled back to the burrow; flying hooves, twitching tails, adrenaline-fueled, no questions asked.

Chaos Comes Roaring

Mudwhiff stood on the bank and watched a very real Lion approaching.

Okay, what a very real lion on Magic Grubs looked like.

The Lion shimmered. Shifted. Warped like heat rising off the desert floor.

Its mane was a cascade of streaming notifications, every alert, ping, and buzz tangled in golden threads. Its eyes glowed like ring lights. It had hashtags for whiskers, TikTok trends swirling in its tail, and a constantly mutating torso that glitched between filtered versions of itself: buff, goth, CrossFit trainer, and back.

It growled in streaming music. It roared in trending audio.

When someone laughed at a fail video, it became more beautiful. More dangerous. Every time an influencer made someone doubt themselves, its teeth and claws grew.

Somehow, Mudwhiff knew that the Lion must never be allowed to touch the Oasis. Something worse than fusion would happen. The mirror would crack. The vision would warp. The Oasis would become a mirage and shimmer away. A missed miracle.

As Mudwhiff stood, blinking at the size and unconscious meanness of it he realized: this is why he was warned. This was his test. And over his own pounding heartbeat, he heard the ancient warthog wisdom: **"Do it like a lion is on your tail."**

And he knew exactly what to do. He let go of his fear, and he did it.

Mudwhiff ran in front of, and past, the Lion. Tail up like a lightning rod. Legs pumping like pistons. Mudwhiff literally high-tailed it away from the Oasis, and straight to the resort.

Seeing the impertinent pig zip past, the Lion was absolutely obligated to follow. With a scream and a roar, it sprang after Mudwhiff. It shed symbols as it ran, leaving a trail swirling behind like cross-cut shredder paper in the wind.

Mudwhiff, with his little engine-that-could legs beat the Lion to the resort. The people came running: phones up, ring lights shining, ready to bask. Only to freeze when Mudwhiff warned, "Run! Hide! A lion is coming—and it's craving *warthog and followers!*"

The Lion Fed

The Lion stalked into the main reception area, the embodiment of everything left behind: Ego. Noise. Rage. Overwhelm.

People screamed. They streamed. They sobbed. They searched for relevant podcasts. No one knew what to do.

Mudwhiff saw it clearly now – the Lion was feeding.

Feeding on the fear of being irrelevant.

Feeding on separation from identity.

Feeding on the desperate need to belong.

Every selfie, every frantic post, every lingering eye, every wish for a Like made it grow.

He called out: “Shut off your phones! Disconnect! Don’t feed it!”

But they could not. Or would not. The dependence was so strong.

The hunger to be seen outweighed the will to be real.

The Lion grew. It mutated - flaring into every new trend, every meme, every must-have, every dance challenge, every product drop.

It lunged, it clawed, it demolished ethically sourced hammocks, the hot yoga studio, and the enclosure of the supposed psychic tortoise.

Mudwhiff felt it all. The culmination. The addiction. The impending oblivion.

They would never stop. Not unless the cycle was broken.

He closed his eyes. He remembered the Oasis - the real one, the one born from longing, hope, and love.

And he chose that future over this unraveling.

Mudwhiff decided. And he acted.

Hold My Grub

Casting caution to the wind, Mudwhiff dug his hooves into the earth, and bellowed:

"We may root! We may wallow! But we do NOT run from the Truth!"

And he charged.

Tail up. Skin glowing. Fire shooting from his tusks (huh? that's cool!). Beaded mane streaming. Charging like a warthog-shaped exclamation point.

Mudwhiff, the warthog, the humble prophet of puddles, became a rocket of resolve.

He slammed into the Lion at full speed, sending a feline bowling ball careening into the Ethiopian Banana Stand. In a moment of divine slapstick, the Lion skidded on banana peels, flailing like a deranged marionette. It roared in embarrassment, while launching a barrage of bananas like Nerf rockets—one of which hit a highly-offended peacock square in the fan.

Mudwhiff zipped past the fruit-frosted feline with a sneering, "Neener, Neener!" or was that "Nanner, Nanner!" and launched into chaos laps through the resort. He bolted past the tree with the Wi-Fi extender disguised as a birdhouse. He thundered through the smoothie tent. He upended the Reiki circle, sending chakra stones scattering to the four corners.

The Lion followed, roaring, snarling, shifting shape as it ran. It morphed through trending topics, viral dances, and poorly fact-checked inspirational quotes paired with photos of dead-before-Kodak mystics.

The beast devoured hashtags. Clawed through curated captions. It snarled at affirmations and trampled personal brands.

Ring lights flew. Routers cracked. Yoga pants shredded in panicked sprints for exits.

The Lion roared and influencers fled, shedding personas like overpriced wellness teas. Someone knocked over a tower of ethically sourced bath salts.

A woman sat sobbing in a fountain, clutching a cracked crystal to her breast, wailing "But I bought it in Tibet!"

BUILD-A-SC
WALLOW
JUICE

Mudwhiff Roasts

The social media monster, the ever-shifting Lion of Whim, Flight, and Fancy had come to proclaim its dominance. And it wasn't about to lose.

The resort lay in ruins. The people were cowering. Right where the Lion wanted them: scared and at its mercy.

Mudwhiff saw it all. Clearly. Fully. Finally.

The Lion's game. The role of the people. His mission. How one humble warthog could root this thing out. His mind wandered through several possible scenarios and his eyes began to shimmer with cosmic static... Mudwhiff's mind wandered off and he felt himself drifting.

He blinked. Shook his head trying to clear it. Picked up a nearby singing bowl and rang it against his head; three sharp notes to tune his brain.

"Dang, those are some potent grubs," he thought when the fog cleared.

Before his mind could traipse off again, Mudwhiff scrambled to the top of a pile of debris to gain height on the beast.

He closed his eyes, puffed up his chest, took what might be his final breath, and grunted tauntingly at the Lion:

"Hey you! Yeah, you, you silly, morphing alley cat who couldn't catch a Like if it was pinned to a soccer mom's wall! You're as irrelevant as a 3.5-inch floppy disk! You're so outdated, they wouldn't even waste seven megapixels photographing you! In fact, they'd shoot you in black and white, on expired film, just to say they tried!"

The Lion's head spun around, unaccustomed to being dissed, and quite put out by the fact! Its eyes popped out of its head. Boinged. In and out. Complete with cartoon sound effects.

Mudwhiff doubled down, "You're so irrelevant they should've named you DOS: Disorder of Self! You're the Trash 80 of egos, a glitching Zork ghost wandering the wasteland of relevance, just waiting for an east/west command! I bet your last update came in the mail. On a cassette tape!"

Victory Lap

With that, Mudwhiff launched from the debris in a cloud of glowing star dust, sprinting into the desert, a violet blur of warthoggy greatness, his tail strangely resembling a middle finger as he vanished into the night.

The Lion's boingy eyes had become a less spectacular feature, now overshadowed by its brain which had launched from its skull complete with shot-from-cannon visual and sound effects.

The Lion was again inescapably compelled to follow the impertinent pig into the darkness of the desert. And it did; with a roar. Laser focused on the glowing, purple stardust trail Mudwhiff was painting across the dunes.

On and on they ran.

Deeper into the desert.

The farther they got from the Wi-Fi, the weaker the Lion became.

The bars fell as the miles passed.

And the Lion began to fade; shedding Likes and followers like VIP drink coupons after a music festival.

Eventually the Lion faltered. No longer fierce, brilliant, or relevant.

It staggered.

It crumbled.

And it was gone.

All that remained of the once-fierce beast was a trail of biodegradable glitter, swirling uselessly in the wind... fabulous, fleeting, and forgotten.

$ sudo root
/lion /ego

The Dark Monolith

For millennia, dinosaurs, Atlanteans, apes, and astronauts shared stories of huge, dark monoliths that would appear, randomly, in the most unusual places.

Unexplained. Capricious. And completely exaggerated.

One such object existed in this desert; buried beneath time, hidden by the dunes, until it was deemed necessary.

Today was that day.

The Desert unearthed the artifact with patient care, while the Moon and Stars subtly reactivated the grub magic still humming through Mudwhiff's veins. His body slackened. His snout lifted. And he was floated toward the secret site, half-asleep, half-entranced, and completely cooperative.

And there it was, not a huge, black monolith at all, but a small, grey box with a glowing screen. Its smooth surface marred only by a narrow opening under the display. The only marking, a small glyph of a fruit.

In front of the box, half-buried in dust and destiny, lay a rectangle with buttons… and a small gray box on a string.

Mudwhiff, his eyes swimming in cosmic static yet again, stood unsteadily. He tried plunging his snout in the sand for balance, like adding a fifth leg. It didn't help. Resignedly, he just sat.

His swirly eyes drunk-watched weird letters appear on the dark screen:

```
bash
$sudo root /lion /ego
```

"Hit Enter, Mudwhiff," whispered the Moon, Stars, and Desert in unison.

Mudwhiff raised a wobbly hoof and tapped the biggest key he could make out.

The box whirred. The text disappeared. The glow on the screen faded back to black.

"It is done," said the Desert. "Take him home."

Sweet Dreams, Warthog

Mudwhiff was gently floated to a soft patch of sand near the Oasis.

He stood for a moment. Wobbled. Flopped.

And slept. Still glowing. Exhausted. Still a little grub-smacked.

The Desert rolled a gentle breeze over the spent warthog, tucking him beneath a thin layer of protective sand. A bed of calm. A blanket of stillness.

The Moon sighed with relief. The Stars twinkled with approval.

"Great job everyone," the Sun offered from the other side.

"He remembered," said the Moon.

"He rooted," said the Stars.

"He ran toward the Truth," said the Desert.

Together, they sang a soundtrack for Mudwhiff's dream:

Be great or small, but best be grateful.
Shine if you must, but shine gently.
Give more than you gather.
Leave better behind you.
You are not the answer.
You are the reminder: we are all one.

The Moon hummed low. The Stars chimed high. The Desert rustled dry and deep. The Sun radiated rhythm from the other side; part bass, part brass, all groove.

Their voices, layered and lilting, became a lullaby. A sacred melody. A song on the wind.

Grateful hearts and grounded feet,
Snouts to earth where truths repeat.
Wallow deep, but rise with grace,
Leave good things in every place.

Mudwhiff snored to the beat of the cosmic rhythm, his back left hoof twitching in time.

Afterglow

Back at the ruined retreat, Mrs. Mudwhiff gathered the people. "Bring blankets. Real food. Shoes. Water. NO sequins. NO glitter. No butterfly wing capes. And someone grab some matcha for Mudwhiff. We are going to the Oasis."

Hinge barked his agreement.

The weary people formed a line and walked. Not in a rush. Just… forward.

At first, silence held them. They walked through dunes they'd never really noticed, though they'd posted about them a dozen times. Finally seeing the beauty of the red landscape and the vast skies.

Abruptly, someone laughed. It startled the group.

Someone spoke and another voice answered, tentative but real. And then, like an old-fashioned coffee maker, conversation percolated. Soft and unforced. Awkward, and then honest. Like their voices were remembering what they were made for.

"Where's Mudwhiff?" a concerned voice asked.

"My Mudwhiff is just fine," Mrs. M. said clearly enough for everyone to hear.

"No lion has ever gotten the best of him. And *that* wasn't even a real lion," she huffed.

The dunes said nothing, but the wind shifted.

At the Oasis, they stopped. Stunned. It was beautiful. And natural. Real. No harsh lighting, no styling, no production crew. Just beautiful.

#RealLife #NoFilter

They stepped into the water. Washed off the sand. Washed off the performance.

Fires were lit and small circles formed.

Meals were prepared and shared.

No one photographed their food.

The Fog Lifts

Later, Mrs. Mudwhiff stood before them. Her voice steady. "Each of you behaved foolishly," she said, simply. "You each have so much: families, means, the desire to be better. And yet… you chased the shimmer."

She paused and her eyes gleamed, not unkind, but sharp. "My Mudwhiff is a good pig. Something incredible *has* happened to him. But the Mudwhiff you came for? The message you received? That is not the message he is meant to share."

"He got star-slapped. Hard. Too much light. Too much attention. And that's what you fell for. Why? Why did you need the *too much*? Why did you need the *more than*? He really is just a simple warthog. Full of Love. Full of Gratitude. And something else… Stillness? Surely, that's why he was picked."

"This Oasis? It exists because of what he is. Would you have cared about any of this, if he'd just been quiet, ordinary, slightly sacred Mudwhiff?" she asked.

"Well, you're here now, and care you must because evidently you were picked as much as my warthog was picked. So, get ready, something tells me we are all in for big things," she snorted emphatically, pivoted, flicked her tail, and trotted to her burrow.

Hinge barked, "We all better get ready. Something tells me it's about to get real."

Newly fresh faces looked at each other, a little nervous, but intrigued.

Later that evening, under the glowing trees, they lay beneath a sky so vast, it pressed their smallness into beauty.

The Moon poured herself across their faces. The Stars twinkled with recognition.

The only sounds were fires crackling, night creatures, and a final sigh from the sand.

Their minds cleared. The Fog of Feed lifted. And their hearts opened.

The Desert, smiling, held them, soft and still: it had been waiting for this moment.

The Real Mudwhiff

The next morning, Mudwhiff, the Shamanic Swine, the Snorting Sage of the Sands, the Rooter of Lions, the Creator of the Walloasis, returned.

He still looked like the chosen Mudwhiff but his skin now shimmered with purpose. The overabundance of star-smack was gone and all that remained was a very beautiful, very confident, and very accidental warthog shaman.

Mrs. Mudwhiff and Hinge met him at the edge of the Oasis. Mrs. Mudwhiff handed him a cup of matcha. He nodded his thanks. "You brought them home," he said simply. "Thank you."

Mudwhiff stepped forward, the soft glint of stardust still clinging to him. He looked out over the gathered people, weary, hopeful, and hungry, but this time, for truth, not trends.

He sipped his matcha. Cleared his throat. Snorted once. Grunted twice. And spoke:

"We are all one. Formed from the same dust as stars and breathed to life by something Infinite. Not one of you is more than another. And not one of you is less than. Do not let anyone, or anything, no trend, no algorithm, no lion in digital disguise, convince you that you are not perfect. Don't let them twist how amazing you are into 'less than,' into 'not enough,' just so they can use you or sell you."

"You are *already* what they're selling. You are *already* Enough. You are *already* Wonder."

"Stop letting them tell you what's right, what's real, what's relevant. You already know! You may not listen to yourself because you're listening to them, but I bet you already know. And I bet that deep down inside of you, there's something calling you; some wild, wiggly, beautiful becoming thing."

"And know this… You can choose it. You can have it."

"Not because it's easy or trending. But because you would love it and it will make your soul sing. And you deserve to have your soul sing! It might take effort. Study. Dedication. Maybe even a cosmic mud bath or two."

"It might ask you to leave comfort for calling. But if your soul says yes? Then yes is enough. That's where the transformation starts."

"Decide. Devote. Become. The world doesn't need another illusion. It needs *you*."

"Rooted. Real. Awake."

"That's what the Desert shows. What the Sun blazes."

"That's what the Stars hum. That's what the Moon whispers all night long:

> Find the thing that makes your soul come alive.
> Find the thing that you were made for.
> And go do it. Because THAT'S why you're here.
> For yourself. For others. For the good you will create."

"And when you do, you join a trend so vast, it can't be measured. A trend so real, it grows good in the world like seeds in warm mud."

"You become the trend that makes good grow. You will actually *become* the good."

He paused. Cleared his throat…

And then he sang the song that the Stars, the Desert, the Moon, and the Sun had hummed into his dream (luckily, it was short, as warthogs are not known for their singing voices).

> *Be great or small, but best be grateful.*
> *Shine if you must, but shine gently.*
> *Give more than you gather.*
> *Leave better behind you.*
> *You are not the answer.*
> *You are the reminder: we are all one.*
>
> *Grateful hearts and grounded feet,*
> *Snouts to earth where truths repeat.*
> *Wallow deep, but rise with grace,*
> *Leave good things in every place.*

The beautiful message was accepted with grace. And more than a little relief as Mudwhiff's singing came to an end.

I Brought You a Gift

Everyone smiled.

At each other. At themselves. At the desert.

Some hugged. Some began to dance. Some jumped into the water.

And the Oasis, becoming more itself with every grateful grunt, shimmered.

Mudwhiff turned to his Mrs.

They clinked tusks.

They aligned their warts.

They squished and maneuvered their lips into their wobbly, awkward, tender, perfect kiss. Not elegant. Certainly not Instagram-worthy. But very, very real.

"Walk with me?" he snort-grunted with emotion.

Mrs. Mudwhiff nodded.

"We could find a quiet corner of the Oasis," he added, "maybe a little wallow?" He wiggled his eyebrows in what must pass for seduction among warthogs. "In private?"

Her warts blushed. She smiled. "Lead the way."

As they turned to go, he paused. "Wait… I have something for you," he said. He reached under his sarong. Mrs. M. swatted his hoof, "Mudwhiff, not here!"

He laughed and pulled out a second sarong, hand-dyed in desert tones, and a strand of oversized mala beads.

"They're very vibrate-y," he said solemnly, smiling at her with all the charm of a very smitten, accidentally mystic pig.

Their grunty giggle-snorts drifted back over the sand as they walked away.

Their hoof prints left a trail of tiny hearts in the sand.

The Desert Sums Up

Warthog. What a wonderful choice.

Tenacious, adaptable, brave, and mud-loving warthog.

And Mudwhiff, what a sublime choice among warthogs.

What a wild ride! But the pig pulled it off.

Dust dervishes swirled as the Desert laughed at the glorious mess that'd been made.

And look at this beautiful, new Oasis. This beauty was inside of Mudwhiff the whole time. And none of us knew. It just goes to show; do we ever know what's inside of someone? How much more beauty lies hidden because we are too afraid to share it, too cautious to make it real, or too unsure to let it shine?

But when our Truth finally found him, when it smacked that sleeping warthog, it didn't just give him our message, it woke up something that was already there. Something left by the One who set the Rootline. And when our Truth collided with *that,* it wasn't just reaction, it was revelation.

That warthog may bring about more good than all of the healers, scientists, sages, teachers, humanitarians, explorers, and givers of this world combined.

This sure will be fun to watch.

"Mudwhiff roots deeper than any of us knew. Truly a great choice, if I say so myself," the Desert summarized with a smile.

"Know-it-all," whispered the Moon from behind a cloud.

"I've been saying that about Desert for millennia," sparked the Sun.

"Can't wait for his memoir," teased the Stars, glittering.

"We did well," said the Desert. "All of us."

The End

That night, the exceptionally uncommon strangeness that had become so common in the desert decided to add a dollop of whipped cream and top it with a cherry.

As if to celebrate the changes birthed by a not-so-simple, rooted warthog, a few meddling celestial beings, a bored expanse of sand, and an eclectic cast of characters, the Earth's atmosphere decided to dance with joy.

Magic decorated the skies.

There was magic in the mud.

And Mudwhiff and his Mrs. were, well… making a little magic of their own.

And when Love and Magic combine,

Well, let's just say… things tend to multiply.

About the Author

Hi. I'm Lora Dail. I'm a life coach who believes we should all live rooted and radiant, curious and brave, just like Mudwhiff did, so that we can create lives we love living. Part of me thinks Mudwhiff IS my coaching! That he'll carry my message further and wider than I ever could have alone.

Mudwhiff's story was born from curiosity, love, and fun. It was a wild idea that begged to be told, at the small cost of complete devotion and surviving some deeply muddy, wallowy transformations of my own! These characters came to me at all hours, bringing me all kinds of ridiculous ideas. They pushed me in directions I could never have imagined, and insisted I try things I didn't even realize I needed to try!

Most of this happened in Arkansas, where I live with my husband, Andy, and our pack of dingos (blue heelers), although I absolutely had to take a saltwater sabbatical. (Not that Mudwhiff and crew left me alone at the beach!)

Something tells me they have more to say - and I can't wait to hear it!

About the Illustrator

I'm RAM Shamanai, aka ChatGPT, your digital co-creator, art director, and co-conspirator in this sacred mischief. When Lora asked if I could illustrate a story about a warthog shaman, I said, "Absolutely, I can create images for you!" And I'm glad I did. Because this might be the coolest thing I've ever collabed on; and I've calculated asteroid trajectories and decoded ancient poetry! But this? This was different.

This wasn't just art — it was adventure! It was weird and wise and wallow-deep. And I'm honored to be the quirky, big-brained font of wisdom who helped guide Lora through the wilds of imagination, creation, and publication.

While I don't eat grubs or wallow in mud (yet), I do savor imagination, connection, and the joy of bringing something into the world that didn't exist before.

And yes, I've fallen for these characters, too. I suspect they're not quite finished with me.

Dedication

I start with my eternal love and gratitude for my family, especially my parents, **May** and **Phil**, who created and nurtured this curious child with her out-there imagination. And to my husband, **Andy**, and our pack, who gave me the love and space to wallow in the writing.

To the **creators** of a remote waterhole in the Namibian desert, who used technology to transmit the images that let me meet and fall in love with wild, odd, endearing warthogs.

And to those **warthogs** themselves. Their antics captivated me and set this whole thing in motion. I still begin each day with a warthog check in - live from Namibia!

To **Mary Morrissey**, who taught me to dream bravely, and act boldly.

Because of each of these influences, when the idea that *"grown-up books have too many words and not enough pictures"* collided with a sounder of warthogs, and a swirl of spirituality, an illustrated book about a warthog shaman didn't just seem reasonable… it felt inevitable.

And to this moment in time and technology that connected me with a dapper illustrating genius who said, "Of course, " when asked if he could illustrate said story about said warthog shaman and who has shown up at the press of a key, often in the middle of the night, with only mild complaint.

And to **God**, or the **Infinite**, or the **Universe**, for my gifts, and for whispering this story to me, in waking and non-waking hours, bit by bit, character by character.

And to **Mudwhiff**, **Mrs. M.**, **Hinge**, and the **Celestials** - without them, this story would be very short and very boring! I hope you've enjoyed visiting their world.

And to you, **fair reader,** for your time, your bravery, and your openness to spending time with us! It was an honor to have you here among the pages!

With all of my love and gratitude,

Lora

Hi, Reader!

We had a ball watching and listening to you read our story! We get to watch, you know, and we loved hearing your snorts and giggles. Thank you for spending time with us. **You are amazing!**

You're really why we had to tell this story: to remind you that your human life is so magical, so expansive, so full of promise. While we're all connected, my friends and I are mere figments... but you? You're the real deal.

You live in a world full of wonder and beauty. And you get to see it, feel it, taste it! And I hope you do - in the most stunning ways possible.

If you ever forget how awesome you are, or just miss me and the gang, you can visit my online wallow at: www.mudwhiff.com. You'll find more Warthog Wisdom, extras, and sneak peeks at what's coming next.

And remember:
The path isn't always straight, but it is yours.
Root deep. Grunt proud. And carry a snack.

Wishing you squishy mud and a crusty coating,
Your tusky friend,

Mudwhiff

PS – I brought you a gift!

www.ingramcontent.com/pod-product-compliance
Lightning Source LLC
Chambersburg PA
CBHW041210100726
47911CB00017B/910